For Geoff and James
with thanks
E.T.

For Grinty
T.M.

SIMON & SCHUSTER BOOKS FOR YOUNG READERS
Simon & Schuster Building, Rockefeller Center, 1230 Avenue of the Americas,
New York, New York 10020. Text copyright © 1992 by Elizabeth Thiel.
Illustrations copyright © 1992 by Terry Milne. First U.S. edition 1993.
Originally published in Great Britain by Heinemann Young Books, a division
of Reed Consumer Books. All rights reserved including the right of
reproduction in whole or in part in any form.
SIMON & SCHUSTER BOOKS FOR YOUNG READERS is a trademark of Simon & Schuster.
Manufactured in Hong Kong

10 9 8 7 6 5 4 3 2 1

Library of Congress Cataloging-in-Publication Data
Thiel, Elizabeth. The polka dot horse / by Elizabeth Thiel :
illustrated by Terry Milne.   p.   cm.   Summary: Afraid of being thrown away,
an old toy horse rolls out into the English countryside and ends up on
a farm where he finds someone to care for him.
[1. Toys—Fiction.   2. Horses—Fiction.   3. England—Fiction.]
I. Milne, Terry, 1964-   ill. II. Title.
PZ7.T3537Po   1993   [E]—dc20   92-10221   CIP
ISBN: 0-671-79419-1

THE POLKA DOT HORSE

by Elizabeth Thiel
illustrated by Terry Milne

SIMON & SCHUSTER BOOKS FOR YOUNG READERS
Published by Simon & Schuster
New York • London • Toronto • Sydney • Tokyo • Singapore

IT WAS SEVEN O'CLOCK on a sunny summer morning when the polka dot horse ran away. No one saw him go, but no one would have cared, for the polka dot horse had grown old.

Once, long ago, he had been the king of the toys, but others had taken his place. He had been tossed to a corner of the garage and forgotten. In time he would be thrown away.

The polka dot horse feared the trash can above all else. And so, on that drowsy Sunday, he decided to escape.

His wooden heart thumped as he rolled along. His wheels rocked and tumbled over the lumpy bumpy lane. And the echo of their clackety-clop rang down into the valley, where sheep and cattle raised their heads to watch the distant figure pass by.

Sometimes he would prick up his ears at the patter of squirrel feet on twigs, or glimpse the bobtail of a rabbit in the shrubs.

And once he saw a pair of marching birds strutting in the sun, their heads cocked, their tails high and proud.

"Where are you going?" shrilled the swallows, wheeling and dipping in the bright blue sky.

But the polka dot horse could only shake his head. "I don't know," he said. And there was a whisper of worry in his soft brown voice.

At length he climbed a grassy slope and reached a tangled hedge.

It was ten times higher than the polka dot horse and covered with brambles and dog roses and wild white flowers that smelled of Christmas trees and summer mornings all rolled into one.

The hedge was broken by a five bar gate that stretched across a stony track. It was open just a crack.

The polka dot horse nudged his nose into the gap and pushed. Then, very slowly, he rolled through.

Before him lay a patchwork world of horses.
Romping in the meadow, rolling in the sun.

And the polka dot horse began to sing inside as he turned to face the downhill path.

He moved slowly at first, wobbling just a little. But the track grew steep, and his wheels lost their grip.

He lurched from side to side, pitching and tumbling, toppling and stumbling on the stones that littered the way.

He closed his eyes in horror as he looked down the slope and saw a tree sprawled across his path.

His front wheels slammed against the trunk and the polka dot horse soared up into the air.

"Help!" he cried as he turned a somersault and fell towards the ground.

But nobody saw him land in a wet and dirty corner of the farmyard. He lay helpless in the deep dank straw, one leg broken and two wheels cracked.

The afternoon faded into homecoming time. The polka dot horse watched through muddy eyes as the hens scuttled up to their roost. He spied the farm cats prowling silently by in search of suppertime treats.

And he lifted his ears when a voice called out, "Jane and Jonathan, come and get your supper!"

He didn't notice the great shaggy shape that crossed the yard to where he lay. But he looked up into the face of a huge farm dog and felt its warm breath on his head.

His dirty, bruised body was rigid with fright as the dog nuzzled his splintered wheels. He tried to squeal, and shut his eyes when the sharp white teeth and panting tongue came close. He thought he might faint when it opened its mouth and picked him up.

The dog trotted slowly across the cobbled yard and into the farmhouse kitchen. It lay down, head between its paws, and dropped the polka dot horse onto the flagstones.

"Yuk! What's that?" Jonathan slid from his chair and peered at the grubby toy.

His mother glanced down. "I expect it's just an old lump of wood. Go away, Bingo. And take that horrible thing with you."

The polka dot horse tried to speak, but his mouth was full of straw. A single dirty tear slid down his nose.

Then suddenly he felt someone lift him from the floor.

Jane laid him gently on her lap. "It isn't a piece of wood, Mom. It's a little horse."

She peeled away a clod of mud and wiggled the broken leg. "He needs a good scrub and some strong glue. I'll clean him up when I've finished my supper."

So she took him to the bathroom where he was bathed in a bubble-filled tub. She washed his mane and tail with proper shampoo and wrapped him in fluffy blue towels. She glued and bandaged his broken leg and mended his rickety wheels.

His white paint gleamed and his glass eyes shone as they had done long ago when he was new. And when Jane held him up to the mirror, he almost laughed and neighed out loud.

The moon was rising as she settled him on a soft cushion and told him to rest and recover.

He dozed, cosy and warm, while she ran downstairs and busied herself in the kitchen.

He slumbered on as she crept through the door and painted quietly in a corner.

But he awoke with a sneeze when she stroked his nose and whispered, "Come and see."

The polka dot horse moved his legs and blinked. He gazed sleepily about the room.

Then a warm glow spread from his middle to his ears and trickled to the tip of his tail.

Next to the bed sat a cardboard box stable, its door wide open, a blanket tucked inside.

And as he snuggled down to dream, he breathed the blissful sigh of a toy that was glad to be home.